Starfish

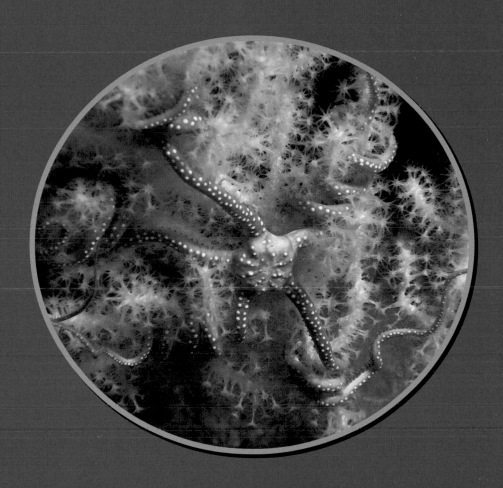

Written by Jo Windsor

Rigby

In this book
you will see
starfish.

You will see:

prickles

arms

feet

2

Look at all the starfish.

Starfish live in the sea.
They like to be in the water.

A starfish can be **orange**.

A starfish can be **blue**.

A starfish can be **red**.

Here is a starfish.

Look at the arms.

This starfish has five arms.

The starfish will...

get food with
its arms   Yes? No?

swim with its
arms   Yes? No?

arms

Here is a starfish on the rocks.

Look at its arms.

This starfish has lots and lots of arms.

arms

Look at this starfish.

Where is its arm?
It is not on the starfish.

The starfish can
grow a new arm.

The starfish has feet on its arms.

This starfish has lots and lots of feet.

The feet help the starfish go over the rocks.

What can go over a rock?

A crab Yes? No?

A starfish Yes? No?

A fish Yes? No?

feet

Look at this!

This starfish is not like a star.

It has no arms at all.

It looks like a ball.

Some starfish have prickles.

prickles

Look at this starfish.

This starfish has
no prickles at all.

Look at this starfish.

It has its food!

A starfish can eat...

a fish Yes? No?

a crab Yes? No?

a mouse Yes? No?

arm

food

Baby starfish look like this.

Baby starfish do not look like starfish at all!

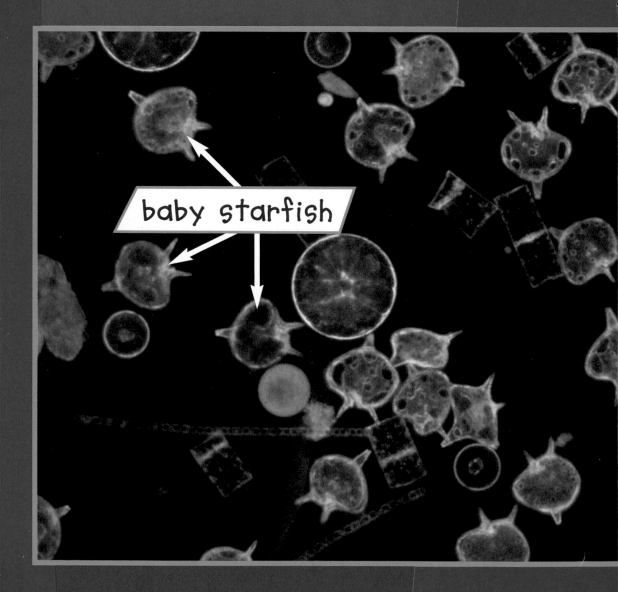